GORGONZOLA
A Very STINKYsaurus

BY

MARGIE PALATINI

ILLUSTRATED BY

TIM BOWERS

KATHERINE TEGEN BOOKS
An Imprint of HarperCollinsPublishers

Library of Congress Cataloging-in-Publication Data is available.
ISBN 978-0-06-073897-6 (trade bdg.) − ISBN 978-0-06-073898-3 (lib. bdg.)

Typography by Allison Limbacher
1 2 3 4 5 6 7 8 9 10   ❖   First Edition

For my spiffed and sometimes

not-so-polished stinkysaurus

—M.P.

To my old CCAD roommates:

Stew, Dave, John Jude, and Craig

—T.B.

Once upon an eon, dinosaurs roamed and ruled.

Some were mighty. Some were fierce. And some were so bad they could scare the socks off you.

But the worst of them all, the *very* worst of them all, was . . .

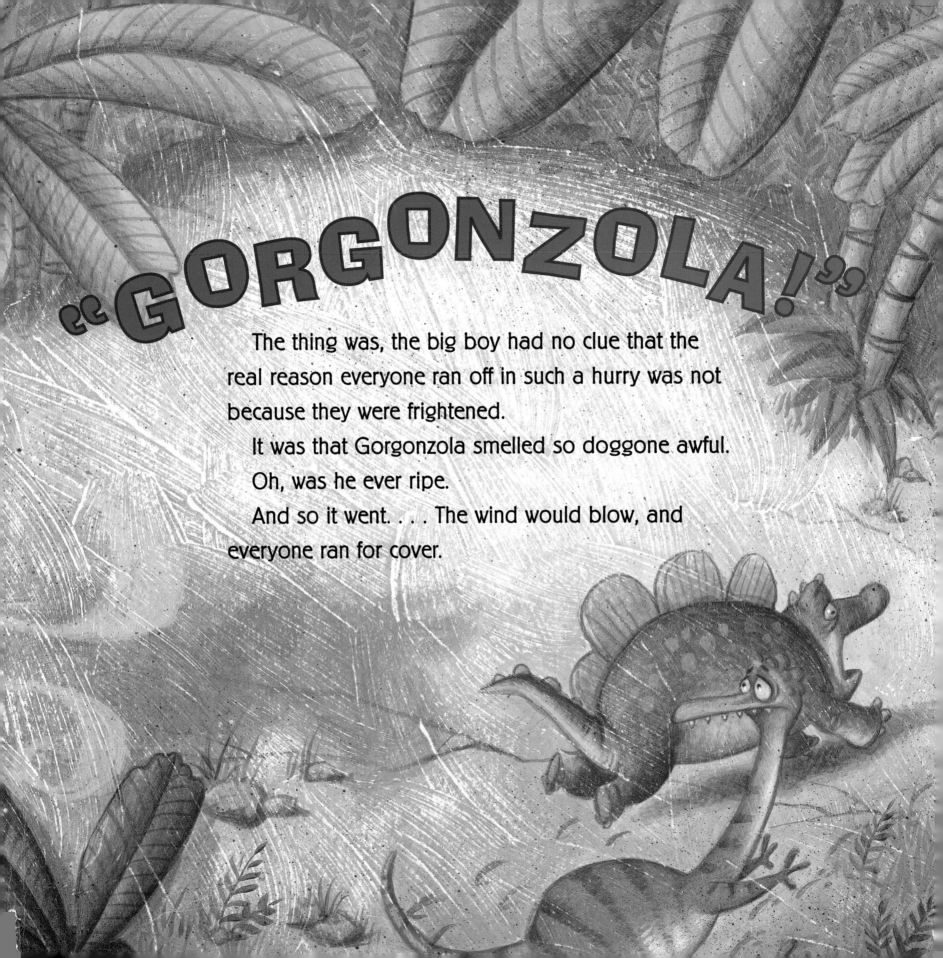

"GORGONZOLA!"

The thing was, the big boy had no clue that the real reason everyone ran off in such a hurry was not because they were frightened.

It was that Gorgonzola smelled so doggone awful.

Oh, was he ever ripe.

And so it went. . . . The wind would blow, and everyone ran for cover.

That is, until one day when one brave little birdie, tired of picking up her nest, **just had enough.**

"Hey, you big stinker. How about a little consideration? Clean up your act, will ya? Nobody's *afraid* of you. We can't stand being *near* you. You're a Primo Stinko! You've got a major dinosaur odor problem."

"Am I getting through to you?"

Gorgonzola was stunned. Shocked.
He took a whiff.
"Wow!" he said with a cross-eyed blink.
"You could petrify a rock with that prehistoric
aroma of yours," the bird squawked.

"Didn't your mother ever tell you about soap, water, or a toothbrush? Yeeesh!"

Gorgonzola gulped. Dinosaur tears rolled down his slimy face and moldy chin. "I was an orphaned egg," he cried. "I hatched myself and have been on my own ever since. I just never had anyone to teach me good hygiene."

"Okay. Stop your blubbering." The bird sighed. She grabbed a couple of leaves and wiped Gorgonzola's runny nose. "Blow."

He snorted and let loose with a slobbering sob. "Dinosaur odor? Honest, I never knew."

"All right already, get a grip," she said with a comforting pat. "So you stink a little . . . okay, a lot. But stop with the waterworks. I'm drowning here."

The bird began to feel a little guilty, a whole lot wet, and more than just a bit sorry for the **stinky** saurus.

"Well, uh . . . I guess . . . if you want . . . I can help you clean up."

"You can?"

The bird fell backward in a faint.

"First—we take care of that breath."

Birdie handed over a large toothbrush, plenty
of toothpaste and stood back a safe distance.

"Okay," she called out from a no-smell zone.
"Go to it!"

Up and down. Back and forth.

"Spit. Spit. **Spit!**"

"And don't forget to floss. You've got stuff
stuck in there from the Mesozoic era. A swish
of mouthwash wouldn't be a bad idea either."

"G-G-G-G-G-G-G-G-GLCH,"

Gorgonzola gargled.

"What do you think? Minty, huh?"

"Not bad," said the bird with a cautious sniff.

She tossed him a sponge and a washcloth.

It was on to the main event. Soap and water.

"Woah! **Woah!** Don't just splash. You gotta scrub, boy! Scrub! Get those shoulders into it. Work it. Work it. And use some shampoo. You're a tad flaky on top."

"OUCH! Oooo! I got soap in my eyes. It's stinging! It's stinging."

"Keep scrubbing, you big baby," said Birdie with a sharp whistle. "Wash behind those ears. And don't forget your neck. You've got about a dozen rings around the collar."

The dinosaur scrubbed and scrubbed.

"Oh, no you don't. Feet first!" ordered the bird. "No playing with bubbles. Get to that toe cheese.

"And . . . a-hem," she whispered. "Remember the tail, buddy."

Gorgonzola remembered everything and, most important, everywhere.

A little powder here.
There. And plenty of lotion
for that scaly skin. Why, he felt like
a new beast. And acted like one too.
"I feel like a real humane being," he said, all
spiffed and polished. "But . . . tell me . . . *exactly*
how often do I have to do this?"

"Well, every day, of course!" Birdie answered.
"That is, if you want to be civilized and hang
around with me and my friends."

Gorgonzola grinned.
"Oh, I do. **I DO.**"

And so he did. He kept clean, and joined
his new friends each Tuesday for bingo.

"BINGO! I win!"

Thursdays for book club.

And Friday was luau night.
He was the life of the party.
And smelled good for it too.

Yes, Gorgonzola was delighted and positively proud to be the first dinosaur officially declared **"ex-stink."**